UFO SPOTTED!

Hilde Cracks the Case

HAVE YOU READ ALL THE MYSTERIES?

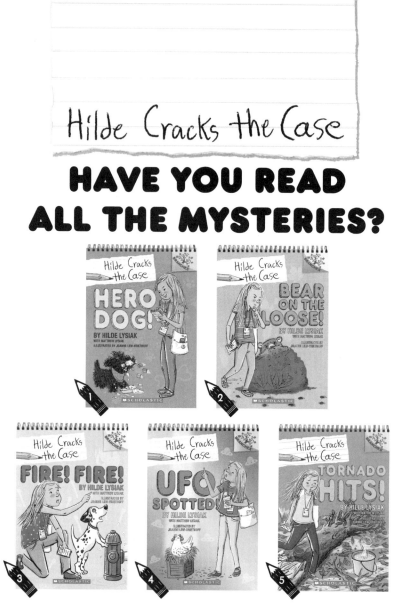

More books coming soon!

scholastic.com/hilde

Hilde Cracks the Case

UFO SPOTTED!

BY HILDE LYSIAK
WITH MATTHEW LYSIAK

ILLUSTRATED BY
JOANNE LEW-VRIETHOFF

BRANCHES™
SCHOLASTIC INC.

To Charlotte and Arabelle, the two best friends
this reporter could have ever asked for.

Copyright © 2018 by Hilde Lysiak and Matthew Lysiak
Illustrations copyright © 2018 by Joanne Lew-Vriethoff

Jacket photos © Dreamstime: Kavee Pathomboon, Frbird; _human/Thinkstock.
Hilde's photo courtesy of Isabel Rose Lysiak.

Photos ©: cover spirals and throughout: Kavee Pathomboon/Dreamstime; back cover Hilde: Isabel
Rose Lysiak; back cover paper: Frbird/Dreamstime; back cover tape: _human/Thinkstock; back cover
paper clip: Picsfive/Dreamstime; 88 paper clips and throughout: Fosin2/Thinkstock; 88 pins: Picsfive/
Dreamstime; 88 bottom: Courtesy of Joanne Lew-Vriethoff; 88 background: Leo Lintang/Dreamstime.

Library of Congress Cataloging-in-Publication Data

Names: Lysiak, Hilde, 2006- author. | Lysiak, Matthew, author. | Lew-Vriethoff, Joanne, illustrator.
Title: UFO spotted! / by Hilde Lysiak, with Matthew Lysiak ; illustrated by Joanne Lew-Vriethoff.
Description: First edition. | New York, NY : Branches/Scholastic Inc., 2018. |
Series: Hilde cracks the case ; [4] | Summary: Selinsgrove is in the grip of alien fever because people
saw a UFO, but nine-year-old reporter Hilde is skeptical about aliens — however, when she and her
photographer sister Izzy find evidence that something crashed near Grove Pond, they are intrigued (and
nervous), and determined to investigate the story for Hilde's newspaper, the *Orange Street News.*
Identifiers: LCCN 2017037060 | ISBN 9781338141641 (pbk.) | ISBN 9781338141658 (hardcover)
Subjects: LCSH: Unidentified flying objects — Juvenile fiction. | Reporters and reporting —
Juvenile fiction. | Detective and mystery stories. | CYAC: Mystery and detective stories. |
Unidentified flying objects — Fiction. | Reporters and reporting — Fiction. | GSAFD: Mystery fiction. |
LCGFT: Detective and mystery fiction.

Classification: LCC PZ7.1.L97 Uf 2018 | DDC 813.6 [Fic] —dc23
LC record available at https://lccn.loc.gov/2017037060

10 9 8 7 6 5 4 3 2 1   18 19 20 21 22

Printed in China 38
First edition, May 2018
Edited by Katie Carella
Book design by Baily Crawford

Table of Contents

Introduction

Hi! My name is Hilde. (It rhymes with *build-y*!) I may be only nine years old, but I'm a serious reporter.

I learned all about newspapers from my dad. He used to be a reporter in New York City! I loved going with him to the scene of the crime. Each story was a puzzle. To put the pieces together, we had to answer six questions: Who? What? When? Where? Why? How? Then we'd solve the mystery!

I knew right away I wanted to be a reporter. But I also knew that no big newspaper was going to hire a kid. Did I let that stop me? Not a chance! That's why I created a paper for my hometown: the *Orange Street News.*

Now all I needed were stories that would make people want to read my paper. I wasn't going to find those sitting at home! Being a reporter means going out and hunting down the news. And there's no telling where a story will take me . . .

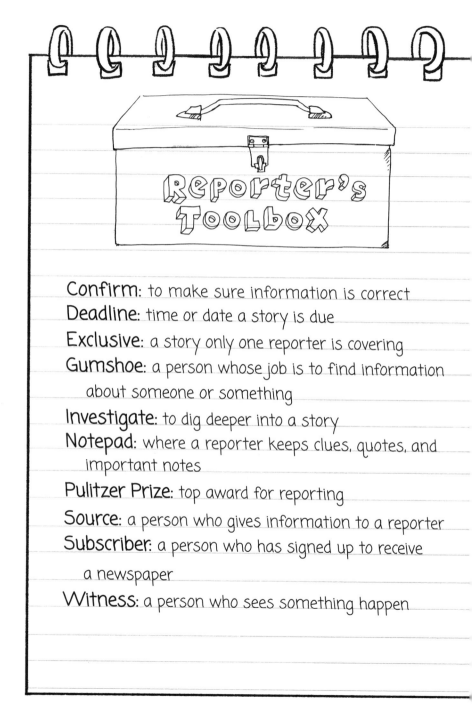

Reporter's Toolbox

Confirm: to make sure information is correct

Deadline: time or date a story is due

Exclusive: a story only one reporter is covering

Gumshoe: a person whose job is to find information about someone or something

Investigate: to dig deeper into a story

Notepad: where a reporter keeps clues, quotes, and important notes

Pulitzer Prize: top award for reporting

Source: a person who gives information to a reporter

Subscriber: a person who has signed up to receive a newspaper

Witness: a person who sees something happen

1 Mysterious Streak of Light

A bright flash of light streaked across the cloudy sky.

My older sister, Izzy, quickly raised her camera.

Click! Click!

"What was that?" I asked.

Izzy looked at her camera screen.

"I don't know," she said. "It moved so fast I didn't get a picture! Do you think it was an airplane?"

I shook my head. "Not any kind of airplane I've ever seen. I'd say it was an unidentified flying object."

"A UFO? You think aliens have landed in Selinsgrove?" asked Izzy.

"Who said anything about aliens? A UFO is just something people see in the sky but do not know what it is,'" I explained.

Whatever it was, it had us both on edge.

Last week we saw a movie at the Grove Cinema. It was called *Spaceship Invaders*. In it, little green men from outer space had landed in a small town. They pretended to be regular people so they could take over the world. It was kind of scary!

Izzy nudged me. "Come on. It looks like it might storm. Let's try to find witnesses before it rains. Maybe someone got a better look at that thing."

She was right.

I needed answers if I wanted to have a story fit for the *Orange Street News*.

Who? What? When? Where? Why? How?

I jotted down a few notes in my notepad.

WHAT: A mysterious flash of
      light in the sky.

WHEN: 3:40 p.m.

"Hilde, look who's coming!" exclaimed Izzy.

The Mean-agers — Donnie, Leon, and Maddy — were walking toward us.

The Mean-agers are a group of Orange Street teenagers known for their rotten attitudes.

Izzy and I stood up.

"What do you guys want?" asked Izzy.

"You two babies don't have a clue, do you?" said Maddy.

"A clue about what?" I asked.

"Did you see that strange light in the sky, too?" added Izzy.

Donnie crossed his arms. "Yup. We saw it. And we know what it was," he said. "But you won't believe us."

"Try us," said Hilde.

"The truth might be too scary for you," added Leon.

2 Alien Invasion?

I knew it was unlikely that the Mean-agers would help us. But a reporter knows that even a bad source sometimes gives good information.

"Tell us what you know," I said.

"Not so fast," said Maddy, looking right at me. "First, you need to promise not to pee your baby diaper!"

Izzy rolled her eyes. "Come on, Hilde," she said. "This is a waste of time. Besides, we don't have all day. We have Pop Pop's surprise birthday dinner tonight, remember?"

Izzy and I needed to get to Benny's Pizzeria by 5:15 p.m. for the party. And my news story had to be posted online by 6 p.m., the usual deadline.

Fortunately, it was only 3:45 p.m.

"We have plenty of time," I told Izzy.

Maddy stepped closer to me. "Well? Do you promise?"

This was going to be humiliating, but I needed to get to the bottom of this story!

I swallowed. "Yes, I promise not to pee my baby diaper," I said softly.

The Mean-agers exploded in laughter.

"Now spill it," I said.

The Mean-agers were quiet.

"Well?" I said.

Finally, Donnie began talking. "That streak of light . . . It was a spaceship from outer space."

I rolled my eyes. "Aliens from outer space aren't real," I said.

"Let's go, Hilde," Izzy said. "They're messing with us!"

"No, it's true," replied Maddy. "And that was not the first spaceship we saw. Earlier today, we saw one flying above Grove Pond!"

Grove Pond was a small, muddy pond at the bottom of Selinsgrove Forest.

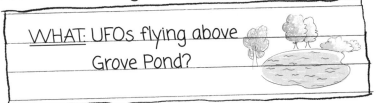

WHAT: UFOs flying above Grove Pond?

"Selinsgrove really *is* being invaded!" said Leon.

A reporter knows that sometimes the truth can be super weird. However, a good reporter knows that you need to stick to the facts.

"How do you *know* the bright lights were spaceships?" I asked.

"The proof is in the field behind the pond," Maddy said.

"What kind of proof?" I asked.

"That's where one of the spaceships crashed," said Donnie.

"Did you see the wreckage?" I asked.

"And risk getting attacked by aliens? Not a chance," said Leon.

Donnie punched his friend's shoulder.

Izzy pulled me aside.

"This is obviously a prank," she whispered.

"Maybe," I answered. "But it's the only lead we have."

I turned to the Mean-agers. "Thanks for the tip. We'll check it out."

Izzy and I hopped on our bikes. "One more thing!" I called out as we pedaled away. "I'm not a baby! But maybe we can find YOU some diapers on our way back!"

"Good one!" said Izzy.

Aliens in Selinsgrove? I knew it was unlikely. But if it *was* true, it wouldn't just be big news for Selinsgrove. It would be big news for *the whole world*!

3 Storm Clouds

Izzy and I sped down Pine Street. The clouds ahead had turned the purple of a bruise. It looked like a big storm was coming.

"What do you think we'll find at Grove Pond?" I asked.

Izzy shrugged. "Maybe nothing. What do you think?"

"Well, I don't think we are going to find little green men," I said. "But I hope we'll find a clue about the UFOs."

We turned right and headed down a bumpy gravel path along the river.

Izzy and I leaned our bikes up against the sign for Grove Pond.

"Maddy said the UFO crashed in the field behind the pond," I said. "Let's check it out."

Izzy and I began walking around the pond.

"I don't see anything here — except some chickens," Izzy said.

"Maybe the UFO crashed at the bottom of this hill," I suggested.

We began hiking down a small, wooded hill.

"If aliens were coming to Earth, why would they want to land here in Selinsgrove?" Izzy asked.

"Maybe they heard about the crispy bacon at the Kind Kat Café?" I joked.

We both laughed. Then my stomach growled. That made me think about tonight's dinner. I couldn't wait to surprise Pop Pop — and to fill my belly with pizza!

I was about to check the time, when Izzy grabbed my arm.

"What's that?" she asked, pointing downhill.

I couldn't believe my eyes.

"Is that . . . ?" I said.

"It can't be!" said Izzy.

4 **The Spaceship**

Izzy and I stood like statues. There were strange pieces of metal scattered all over the hillside!

"This must be where the spaceship crashed!" said Izzy.

The pieces were the size of bent cookie sheets and looked just as hard and shiny.

I walked over to the wreckage. "Well, *something* definitely crashed here. But I don't see anything that proves it came from outer space."

Izzy began taking pictures. *Click! Click!*

I took some notes.

WHAT: Strange pieces of metal?

WHERE: Hillside behind Grove Pond.

I bent down to touch a piece of metal, but Izzy smacked my arm.

"What are you doing?!" she shouted.

"I thought it would be a good idea to bring a piece home to investigate," I said.

"Are you out of your mind? Remember that space invaders movie?" Izzy said. "If this wreckage *is* from a different planet, it could carry an alien disease."

"I hadn't thought about that," I replied. "Just to be safe, I guess we can take a closer look at your pictures later."

"Good plan," Izzy said.

I looked at my notepad.

"So the only fact we have is that there was a bright flash in the sky," I said. "Maybe two flashes, if we believe the Mean-agers."

"Their story seems true now that we've found this crash site," added Izzy.

"Right," I said. "But we need a lot more information if we are going to uncover *where* this wreckage came from. And if these pieces of metal really *are* from a spaceship, then we could be working on a Pulitzer Prize–winning story."

"That's great!" said Izzy. "Now can we get out of here?"

Just then, we heard footsteps.

We jumped behind the closest tree to hide.

"It's the aliens!" Izzy cried.

5 The Green Hand

Izzy and I crouched behind the tree trunk. We stayed perfectly still so that whoever — or whatever — was coming wouldn't know we were there.

"The aliens have come to get their spaceship," Izzy whispered.

The footsteps kept coming. They were getting closer when, suddenly, they stopped.

"Can you take a peek with your camera?" I whispered.

"No way!" she said. "I don't want whatever is out there to see *me*!"

I rolled my eyes. "Some big sister you are."

Izzy shrugged.

Even though I didn't want to admit it, I felt scared, too. But was I really going to let my fear get in the way of reporting the news?

"We're being silly," I said.

"Hilde, remember," Izzy whispered, "reporters should not become part of the story. And if you get zapped up in an alien spaceship, then that is exactly what will happen. Except no one will be here to write it!"

Zapped up in a spaceship? Now this was getting ridiculous.

"Don't be such a scaredy-cat," I said, standing up. "There is no such thing as aliens."

My heart was pounding. I took a deep breath and peeked around the tree.

No one was there.

"See, Izzy, I told you there was nothing to be —" I started to say. But then my jaw dropped.

I could see part of someone — or something — picking up a piece of metal on the hillside!

I ducked back behind the tree.

"What is it, Hilde? What did you see?" asked Izzy.

"I-I-I saw a hand," I stammered.

"Why are you afraid of a hand?" she asked.

I tried to talk, but it felt like my mouth was full of marbles. "The hand — it was green!!"

6 Don't Look Back!

"You saw a *green* hand?" Izzy repeated. Her eyes were the size of silver dollar pancakes.

"Yes!" I said, my voice shaking.

"Hilde, *aliens* are green!" Izzy said. "Let's make a run for it!"

Izzy and I ran back up the hill as fast as we could.

"I can see our bikes!" I yelled.

As we sprinted around the pond, I risked a quick glance behind us.

"No one is chasing us," I said, slowing down.

I had never run so fast in my life!

I stopped to catch my breath. Out of the corner of my eye, I saw Izzy looking back behind us.

"What's wrong?" I asked.

"My camera," she said. "I left it behind the tree."

Izzy had saved her allowance for *two years* to buy her camera.

"We have to go back!" I said. "I know how much you love that camera. Besides, I'd rather deal with aliens than with Dad after he finds out you lost it."

Izzy shook her head. "We can't go back, Hilde!"

"We can't leave it there. We need those photos!" I argued.

Izzy sighed. "What if we come back for it in a little bit? You know, after the alien is gone."

I checked my phone. It was already 4:30 p.m.

"Okay," I replied. "But a green hand isn't proof of aliens."

"Where should we go next?" Izzy asked.

"We need to find more facts," I said.

I had an idea. A reporter knows that speaking to an expert can be a great way to move a story forward. So we just needed to find an expert.

"Can you think of anyone in Selinsgrove who would know a lot about aliens and spaceships?" I asked.

"Maybe Walter?" Izzy suggested. "He knows a lot about everything."

Walter could sometimes be cranky, but he read a lot of books. He even owned a bookstore.

"Great idea!" I said. "Maybe he can help us understand what these UFOs *really* are."

Izzy and I pedaled up Pine Street. We were about to turn right on Market Street when we ran into our friends Myah and Lexie. They went to Selinsgrove Middle School.

Izzy and I hopped off our bikes.

"Hey there!" I said.

Myah and Lexie didn't answer. They looked us up and down.

"Is something wrong?" asked Izzy.

Myah and Lexie were usually giggly, but not now. They looked serious.

"Why aren't you two saying anything?" I asked.

Finally, Myah spoke. "Are you both . . . human?"

7 Aliens among Us?

Izzy and I stared at Myah and Lexie.

"Are we both *human*?" I asked. "What kind of question is that?"

Izzy stepped closer to the girls. "*I* am a human. But I have always wondered what planet Hilde came from," she joked.

"The planet Awesome!" I shot back.

Lexie laughed. Then she turned to Myah. "It's okay. It's really Izzy and Hilde."

"Who else would we be?" I asked.

Myah raised her eyebrows. "Haven't you heard? Aliens are taking over Earth — and they're starting with Selinsgrove!"

"Aliens are pretending to be people!" added Lexie.

I knew a reporter needed to keep an open mind, but an alien invasion still seemed *really* far-fetched.

"What makes you think aliens are taking over people?" I asked as I took out my notepad.

"Well," said Myah. "We ran into Mrs. Hooper, who said she overheard Mayor Jeff talking to —"

I interrupted her. "I need facts. Not rumors. Did you two actually *see* any aliens?"

"Well, no," said Lexie. "But everyone has been acting weird ever since that bright light flashed across the sky earlier today."

"How are people acting weird?" I asked.

"Glenn at the Kind Kat Café couldn't remember my name today," answered Lexie.

"And I saw Officer Dee chasing Professor Henry," added Myah. "They were both staring at the sky. I thought they were going to bang into each other!"

Professor Henry taught at Selinsgrove University — and he was a subscriber to the *Orange Street News*. I knew from delivering his paper that he lived on Eighth Street.

"Has anyone you've talked to actually *seen* aliens?" I asked.

Myah and Lexie looked at each other.

"I guess not," said Lexie.

I looked down at my notepad. It was full of wild theories, but thin on facts. Not good.

Izzy and I needed to get moving.

"Thanks for the tips," I said.

I turned to Izzy as we walked away. She was biting her lip.

"Don't tell me you believe people are being taken over by aliens?" I said.

"I'm not sure what to think," she said. "How do you explain the mysterious light in the sky? Or the strange pieces of metal? Or the green hand? I mean, you always say sometimes the truth is super weird."

"Sure. But *weird* is one thing. *Unbelievable* is another. I also always say that the first thing a reporter needs to do is get all the facts," I said. "Let's go talk to Walter. Maybe he'll have some answers for us."

We biked down Market Street and pulled up to WALTER'S BOOKS.

8 Smartest Person in Town

A bell above the door clanged as we walked inside the bookstore.

Walter was sitting behind the counter. In one hand, he held a book. In the other, a steaming mug.

"Hilde, he looks like he doesn't want to be bothered," Izzy whispered.

"He always looks like that," I answered. "But we have a deadline to meet."

I stepped up to the counter.

"Hi, Walter," I said.

He kept reading.

"Hi, Walter!" I said again, louder.

Walter lowered his book and glared at us. "I am not hard of hearing. I heard you the first time. What can I help you with?"

"We're sorry to bother you," Izzy said.

"I was wondering if I could ask you a few questions," I said.

"Hmmm," he said. "Is this for that paper of yours?"

I stood up straighter.

"As a matter of fact, it *is* for the *Orange Street News*," I said. "We are working on a story about UFOs. We were hoping you could tell us if aliens are real."

Walter put down his book.

"Aliens?" he repeated. He rubbed his beard. "Now, why do you think I would know anything about aliens?"

"Because everyone says you're the smartest person in town," answered Izzy.

"That may be true," Walter said. "But I am the smartest because I know what I *don't* know. And I certainly know not to discuss things I don't know."

His words confused me. I tried again. "So do you *know* if aliens are real?"

Walter leaned forward. "Do you girls know how big the universe is?"

We shook our heads.

"This universe is bigger than you could ever imagine," he said. "So anyone who is *sure* our planet is the only one that has life on it — well, no one will be calling *that* person the smartest person in Selinsgrove. I can tell you that."

"That makes it sound like you *do* believe in aliens," said Izzy.

"I believe that — in a universe as big as ours — it is unlikely we are alone," he answered.

My phone vibrated. But it is rude to look at your phone during an interview, so I ignored it.

Then I heard Izzy's phone vibrate, too. She glanced at the text.

"Dad wants us home right away," Izzy said.

"Sorry, Walter," I said, "but we've got to go."
Walter picked up his book.

I checked my phone as we rushed out. It was only 5 p.m., so it wasn't time for Pop Pop's party yet.

Izzy and I jumped on our bikes.

"I wonder what could be wrong?" I asked.

"I don't know. But Dad's text was in ALL CAPS, so we'd better hurry!" said Izzy.

COME HOME RIGHT AWAY.

 9 Deep Trouble!

Dad was standing in the doorway. He looked angry. And he was holding Izzy's camera.

"My camera!" Izzy exclaimed.

"Umm . . . Hi, Dad!" I said cheerfully.

"Do you girls have something you want to tell me?" he asked. "Like what this *very* expensive camera was doing behind Grove Pond?"

Izzy stammered. "W-we were investigating a story, and I accidentally left it there."

"Well, you are lucky Professor Henry found it. And it's a good thing you wrote your name on the camera strap," Dad said. "But you need to take better care of your things."

"I'm sorry," said Izzy.

We sat down on the couch.

Dad handed her the camera.

"Let me guess," he said. "You're investigating the mysterious lights in the sky?"

I quickly pulled out my notepad. "Yes! What have you heard?"

He smiled. "Sorry, no facts. Only rumors."

I frowned.

Dad ruffled my hair. "Oh, there's been a slight change of plans for Pop Pop's party. We've moved dinnertime from five fifteen to six."

I checked the time. It was 5:10 p.m.

"So we have fifty minutes before we have to be at Benny's?" I asked.

"Yes," Dad said. "You can go back to investigating. Just don't be late."

"We'll be there on time," I promised as Dad headed upstairs. "We can't wait to surprise Pop Pop and give him the special gift we made!"

Izzy turned to me. "Let's take a closer look at those metal pieces now that I have my camera back."

"That's a great idea!" I said.

Izzy pulled the pictures up right away.

"Look!" I said, pointing. "There are some sort of markings stamped on that piece . . ."

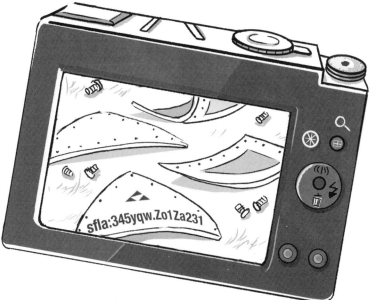

Izzy zoomed in.

"Do you think those numbers and letters could be a secret alien code?" Izzy asked.

"I doubt it. But they're definitely a clue, so I'll write them down," I said. "And I think now is a great time to review our notes."

I opened my notepad.

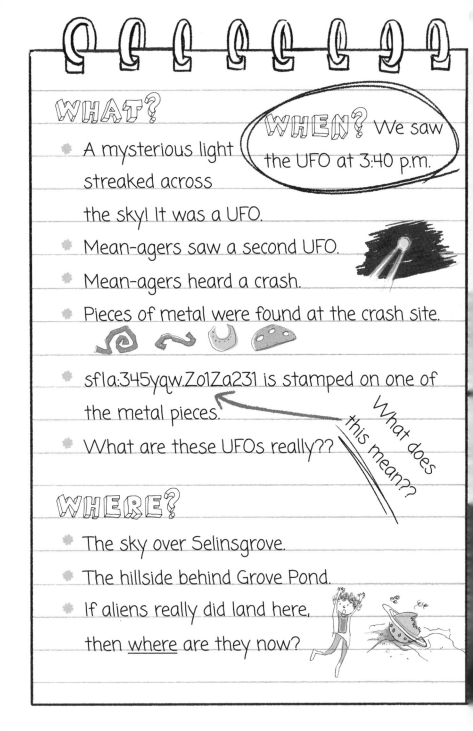

WHAT?

- A mysterious light streaked across the sky! It was a UFO.
- Mean-agers saw a second UFO.
- Mean-agers heard a crash.
- Pieces of metal were found at the crash site.
- sfla:345yqw.Zo1Za231 is stamped on one of the metal pieces.

  What does this mean??
- What are these UFOs really??

WHEN?

We saw the UFO at 3:40 p.m.

WHERE?

- The sky over Selinsgrove.
- The hillside behind Grove Pond.
- If aliens really did land here, then <u>where</u> are they now?

WHO?

* Aliens? (I saw a green hand! Whose hand was it?)
* Who else could be flying these UFOs?

HOW? HOW ARE THESE UFOs FLYING?

* Using top secret alien technology?
* Something else?

Walter believes aliens could be real.

WHY?

* Did aliens crash here by accident on their way to somewhere else?
* Do aliens want to take over people, like Myah and Lexie said?
* Or is there a reason for the UFOs being here that is <u>NOT</u> connected to aliens??

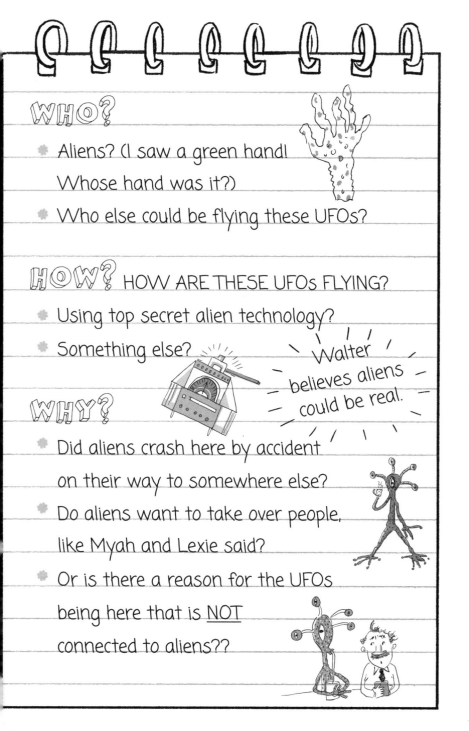

"UGH!" I said. "We aren't even close to having a story. We need FACTS! There must be *someone* who knows what's going on!"

"What about Professor Henry? He must've been on the hillside this afternoon if he found my camera," Izzy said. "And didn't Lexie say she saw him staring at the sky earlier?"

"You're right! He could be a witness," I said.

"Or HE could be an alien," answered Izzy.

"I wouldn't go that far," I said. "But I do have a feeling Professor Henry may be right in the middle of this mystery. Let's go see him!"

"We should have just enough time," Izzy
agreed. "But then we need to head to Benny's."

Izzy put Pop Pop's gift in her backpack.

We ran outside, hopped back on our bikes,
and headed down Orange Street.

10 Knock! Knock!

We pedaled to Professor Henry's house.
"It sure got dark quickly," said Izzy.
"It looks like it might storm soon," I said.
After two short blocks, we skidded to a stop.
"This is the house," I said.
"The lights are off," Izzy said, frowning.
We knocked on the door.

No one answered.

"I guess he isn't home," I said.

Izzy started to head back to our bikes. She stopped.

"Hey, the garage light is on," she said. "Maybe he's in there."

We followed the path to the garage and knocked on the door.

"Professor Henry!" Izzy called out. "Are you in there?"

Again, no one answered.

I stood up on my tippy-toes to peek in the window.

I gasped. "Izzy!" I cried. "Look what's in the corner of his garage!"

Shiny, bent pieces of metal were piled high in Professor Henry's garage.

"Those look like the same pieces of metal we saw at the UFO crash site!" said Izzy.

My hand was shaking as I jotted down some notes. This was a BIG clue!

Izzy took a picture.

"I told you Professor Henry was an alien!" she said. "Well, or could he be working for the aliens?"

"I don't know what to think," I said. "But I need to get a closer look. We need to make sure those pieces have the same markings on them as the pieces from the wreckage. Can you zoom in on one?"

Izzy looked at her camera screen. We held our breath as she zoomed in . . .

The tiny letters and numbers were EXACTLY the same!

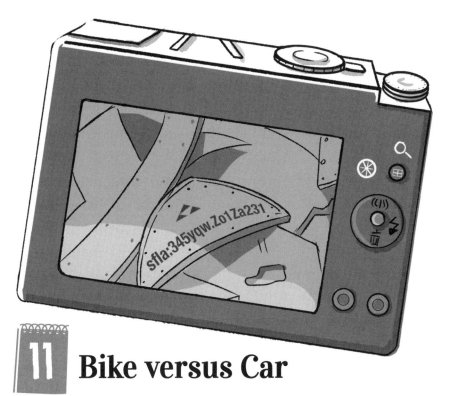

11 Bike versus Car

We knew that Professor Henry had been at the UFO crash site and now we knew pieces of metal from the site were in his garage. He was definitely involved . . . But how?

"Without interviewing Professor Henry, we don't have enough facts for a story," I said.

"What do you mean?" asked Izzy. "*Obviously*, he's helping the aliens rebuild their spaceship!"

"I can't write a story without all the facts," I argued. "We still don't know that the wreckage came from an alien spaceship."

"But this story is HUGE!" Izzy cried. "You need to post it now! We are about to miss our deadline!"

I checked the time.

"We've already missed it," I said, frowning. "But a reporter knows it is more important to be right than to be first. We can't rush this story."

Izzy crossed her arms. I knew she was upset.

But then her jaw dropped. "Hilde, it's after six p.m.?!" she cried.

"Oh, no! We're late for Pop Pop's party!" I said.

Just then, we saw Dad's car whiz by. Pop Pop was in the passenger seat.

I smiled at Izzy. "Good thing Pop Pop's always late, too!"

As we hopped on our bikes, Izzy called out, "Yeah! But we still need to beat them to the restaurant! I know a shortcut. Follow me!"

Izzy hopped the curb, crossed Orange Street, and then cut through Rotary Park.

My sister was always fast on a bike, but I had never seen her pedal *this* fast! It was hard to keep up.

"Benny's is straight ahead!" I shouted.

We looked both ways. Dad's car was stopped at the red light.

"Hurry!" said Izzy.

Somehow, we crossed Market Street without being spotted.

"We did it!" I cheered.

Izzy smiled.

We were running our bikes to the back of the restaurant when we heard a familiar voice.

"Hey!"

I looked up. It was Mom. She was ducking down behind a chair.

The patio was decorated. My little sisters, Georgie and Juliet, were there. Even my mimi was crouching down behind some balloons.

"You girls are just in time!" said Mom.
Izzy and I crouched down beside her.

Soon, the patio door opened.
We all jumped out of our hiding spots.
"Surprise!" we yelled.

12 UFO Chase!

Pop Pop jumped. Then he let out a big laugh.

"Is all this for me?" he said.

"Happy birthday!" we shouted.

Two waiters came out. They each set down a large pizza.

We dug right in. I was about to grab a second slice, when a flash of light streaked across the sky.

"Another UFO!" I cried.

"It's flying behind Grove Pond again!" said Izzy.

"Oh, my!" said Mom.

"That is unbelievable!" Dad said.

Pop Pop stepped over to Izzy and me. "I ran into Mr. Troutman at the grocery store and he said people have been acting funny since those strange lights appeared," said Pop Pop.

"Oh, that Mr. Troutman is just a gossip," answered Mimi.

"Well, I think *not* being able to explain these strange lights has caused a lot of people to act weird," I said.

"These girls need to find the facts," Pop Pop agreed.

"It's time for us to crack this case wide open!" I said.

Izzy and I looked at Mom and Dad.

"Don't even think about it," Dad said sternly.

"You aren't leaving," Mom added. "Not on your grandfather's birthday."

Pop Pop looked at us and smiled. He turned to Mom and Dad. "I suppose because it's *my* birthday, I can get what I want . . . right?" he said.

"Of course," Dad answered.

"Well, my birthday wish is that these two gumshoes get to the bottom of this story!" Pop Pop said. "I can't wait to read a fact-based front-page story that solves the Selinsgrove UFO mystery!"

I grabbed my tote bag. Izzy grabbed her camera and her backpack.

We looked at Dad. He shrugged and smiled.

"Thanks, Pop Pop!" we said, giving him a quick hug.

Then Izzy and I biked down Pine Street like we had been shot out of cannons.

I looked up. The UFO was moving in a zigzag motion toward Grove Pond.

"Hurry!" I yelled. My eyes were glued to the dancing yellow light in the sky. "We have to get there while the UFO is still up in the sky!"

Izzy and I turned onto the gravel path. It was dark. I squinted to see where I was going.

"Pedal faster!" Izzy shouted.

I looked up again. The light was becoming clearer now. It wasn't just one light. It was several lights. And they were spinning!

I strained my eyes upward, trying to see

more. But my gaze was broken by Izzy screaming: "Hilde, look out!"

I jolted my eyes back down to look at the path. I was headed right for the pond!

I slammed on my brakes, but it was too late!

SPLASH!

"Yuck!" I screamed.

Grove Pond wasn't very deep, but when I tried to climb out, my feet wouldn't move. They were stuck in the muddy bottom!

"Quick, Izzy!" I said. "Give me a hand!"

Izzy dropped her bike and grabbed a large stick. She stretched it toward me.

"Grab on!" she said.

I reached for the stick.

"I can't get it!" I yelled.

Suddenly, the UFO stopped zigzagging.

It hovered in midair right above us! We were standing in a bright circle of light.

"We found the UFO!" I said.

"Or the UFO found us!" Izzy shouted. "I've seen enough movies to know THIS IS IT! The aliens are going to take us in their spaceship!"

13 Lights from Above

I tried to look up, but the lights were blinding.

"Hold out the stick, Izzy!" I shouted. "Hurry!"

Izzy scooted closer to me.

I used all my strength, stretching my arm as far as it would go. Finally, I grabbed the stick.

Izzy pulled me out of the swampy pond, and I scrambled onto dry ground.

The UFO was hovering above us. It was making a loud buzzing noise.

I pulled out my notepad.

Izzy grabbed her camera. She aimed it at the UFO.

Then the UFO started flying down closer and closer. I was seeing spots from staring up at the light.

"AHHH!" I screamed as something sharp scratched my foot.

I looked down. Within the circle of light, I could see a strange claw reaching toward me, trying to grab my foot.

I jumped to get away from the claw.

Then I blinked and looked back down at the ground. We were surrounded by chickens!

They were scampering in all directions.

"The lights must be scaring them, too!" said Izzy.

BUZZZZ! The UFO's buzzing sound got louder as the craft got closer to the ground.

Then we saw a shadow. This time, it wasn't chickens. It wasn't even the UFO.

Izzy grabbed on to me.

A figure stepped into the light!

14 Full of Hot Air!

The body standing before us was GREEN! But we couldn't see its head. It was still outside the circle of light.

"Are you girls okay?" a voice asked.

"The alien speaks our language!" said Izzy.

"Wait, I know that voice," I said. "Step into the light."

The figure wasn't an alien, it was — Professor Henry! He was wearing a green suit and holding a large remote control.

Professor Henry pressed some buttons on the remote. The UFO came down and — THUD! It landed beside us. The lights turned off.

Izzy and I stared at the object. It looked a lot smaller on the ground than it did in the sky!

"Do you like my drone?" Professor Henry said, smiling.

"Your what?" Izzy asked.

"My drone. It's like a small remote-controlled airplane," he explained.

"Why are you flying a drone?" I asked.

"I'm doing a study on the environment for Selinsgrove University," he explained. "This is a weather balloon drone. It collects information like temperatures and the amount of water in the air. Hopefully, the data this drone collects will help people better predict when the next big storm might come. And since it looked like it might storm today, I wanted to collect as much information as I could."

I wrote everything down. I had some great quotes!

"That all makes sense," I said.

"Yeah," Izzy agreed. "But why are you dressed like that?"

"Well, whenever I'm working on a scientific study, I like to make sure I am fully covered. This way, if I have to dig around in a muddy pond like this one — maybe to search for a drone that crashed — I can stay safe and clean. I'm also often working outside in stormy weather, so this suit keeps me dry."

"Oh," I said. Then Izzy and I started laughing. We couldn't stop.

"What's so funny?" asked Professor Henry.

"A lot of people saw the lights in the sky and thought . . ." I began.

"And when Hilde saw your *green* hand . . ." Izzy added.

"Everyone thought my drone was an alien spaceship?" he said.

Professor Henry started laughing, too. "Oh, geez! I heard people talking about aliens, but I had no idea they were talking about my drones! I guess Officer Dee didn't tell anyone what I was doing."

"Don't worry," I said. "That's what the *Orange Street News* is for. We'll let people know the truth."

Izzy took pictures of the drone.

I stepped in for a closer look. This drone had a new set of letters and numbers on it.

"What is this code for?" I asked Professor Henry.

"That's a serial number," he replied. "Each drone has its own marking. That way, I can keep track of which piece of equipment is which."

Izzy took a close-up shot of the serial number. *Click!*

"Oh — I almost forgot!" she said. "Thank you for bringing my camera back!"

"Of course." Professor Henry smiled. "I found it while I was cleaning up my drone that crashed."

Izzy turned to me. "That explains the metal pieces we saw in his garage. Mystery solved!" she said. She slapped me five.

As happy as I was that we had gotten our story, I couldn't help but feel sad. We had missed Pop Pop's party . . . We never even gave him our special present.

Just then, a new set of light beams shined on us.

I shielded my eyes.

15 Bird's-Eye View

This time, the bright lights weren't coming from above. They were coming from the gravel path. Car doors swung open. Dad, Mom, Georgie, Juliet, Mimi, and Pop Pop piled out.

"Boy, are we glad to see you guys!" I said.

Izzy and I quickly explained how the mysterious UFOs were actually Professor Henry's weather balloon drones.

Professor Henry nodded.

Dad smiled. "Nice job!" he said.

"Great investigative reporting!" Mom added.

Pop Pop held out two slices of cake. "You didn't think I would forget to save my sweet-toothed granddaughters birthday cake, did you?"

Izzy and I smiled. Then Izzy handed him our gift.

"Happy birthday, Pop Pop," we both said.

He ripped off the paper.

"The *Pop Pop Post*!" he said, reading the front page.

"Izzy and I made you a special newspaper full of stories and pictures of our favorite memories together," I explained.

"This is the best gift ever," Pop Pop said, smiling.

Izzy and I dug into the cake.

Then we posted our news story online. Better late than never!

Professor Henry walked over. "Would you girls like to fly my drone?"

"Yes!" we shouted.

Izzy picked up the remote control. The drone lifted into the air. "It's like driving a remote control car — but in the air!" she said.

A screen on the remote was connected to a camera on the drone. It gave us a bird's-eye view of Selinsgrove.

"Cool!" I said.

Professor Henry pointed to numbers on the screen. "This number shows how fast the wind is blowing and this one shows the temperature."

Izzy pushed a button. The drone flew higher and higher.

"The numbers are going crazy," said Izzy. "The wind is pushing the drone all around. I'm losing control!"

Professor Henry took the remote.

When he looked at the screen, his eyes nearly bulged out of his head.

"Oh, my!" he cried. "Sorry, girls, but I have to go!"

Professor Henry ran off.

"I wonder what that was about," said Izzy.

"I don't know, but it sure seems like his drone saw something BIG," I replied. "The people of Selinsgrove count on the *Orange Street News* to get the facts. So, let's go get 'em!"

I pulled out my notepad.

UFO MYSTERY SOLVED![1]

BY HILDE KATE LYSIAK

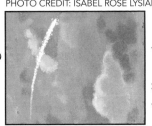
PHOTO CREDIT: ISABEL ROSE LYSIAK

The mysterious light in the sky that many Selinsgrove residents thought was a spaceship turned out to be a weather balloon drone.[2]

Residents saw the first bright light streak across the sky above Grove Pond at 3:40 p.m. The mystery deepened after metal pieces were found on a nearby hillside. Many residents thought the unidentified flying object was an alien spaceship. However, an *Orange Street News* investigation revealed that the UFOs were actually weather balloon drones that belonged to Professor Henry of Selinsgrove University.[3]

"Oh, geez! I heard people talking about aliens, but I had no idea they were talking about my drones!" Professor Henry told the *Orange Street News.* [4]

Professor Henry uses information from these drones to learn more about the weather. [5]

"I'm doing a study on the environment," Professor Henry told the *Orange Street News.* "Hopefully, the data this drone collects will help people better predict when the next big storm might come." [6]

PHOTO CREDIT: ISABEL ROSE LYSIAK

1. HEADLINE 2. LEDE 3. NUT 4. QUOTE 5. SUPPORT 6. KICKER

WHO? Hilde Lysiak

WHAT? Hilde is the real-life publisher of her own newspaper, the *Orange Street News*! You can read her work at www.orangestreetnews.com.

WHEN? Hilde began her newspaper when she was seven years old with crayons and paper. Today, she has millions of readers!

WHERE? Hilde lives in Selinsgrove, Pennsylvania.

WHY? Hilde loves adventure, is super curious, and believes that you don't have to be a grown-up to do great things in the world!

HOW? Tips from people just like you make Hilde's newspaper possible!

Matthew Lysiak is Hilde's dad and coauthor. He is a former reporter for the *New York Daily News*.

Joanne Lew-Vriethoff was born in Malaysia and grew up in Los Angeles. She received her B.A. in illustration from Art Center College of Design in Pasadena. Today, Joanne lives in Amsterdam, where she spends much of her time illustrating children's books.

Hilde Cracks the Case

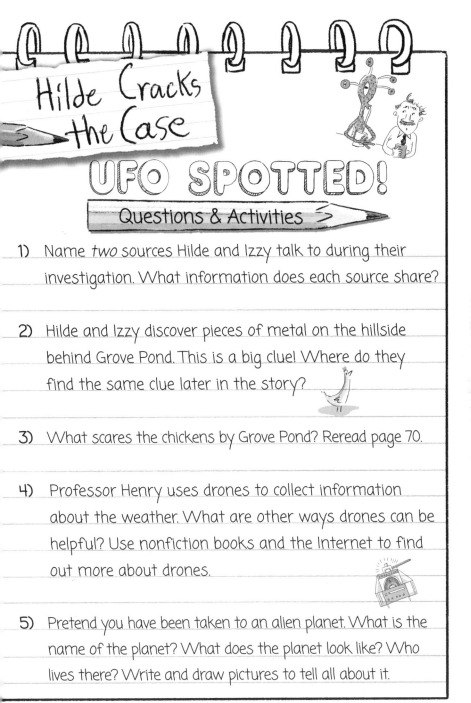

UFO SPOTTED!

Questions & Activities

1) Name *two* sources Hilde and Izzy talk to during their investigation. What information does each source share?

2) Hilde and Izzy discover pieces of metal on the hillside behind Grove Pond. This is a big clue! Where do they find the same clue later in the story?

3) What scares the chickens by Grove Pond? Reread page 70.

4) Professor Henry uses drones to collect information about the weather. What are other ways drones can be helpful? Use nonfiction books and the Internet to find out more about drones.

5) Pretend you have been taken to an alien planet. What is the name of the planet? What does the planet look like? Who lives there? Write and draw pictures to tell all about it.